The Great TORTOISE&HARE Counting Race

MELISSA MATTOX • MICHAEL TERRY

"I'm counting," says Tortoise.

"Counting? I **love** to count!"

"Me too! Now, please don't interrupt," says Tortoise. "**4, 5, 6** ..."

"**7, 8, 9**!" Hare shouts, bouncing up and down. "And... wait, what comes after **9**?"

"**10**," says Tortoise, "but don't count so fast."

But Hare doesn't listen.

"11, 12, 13, 14..." giggles Hare.

"Wait!" Tortoise shouts.

"Be patient," says Tortoise. "I'm getting there."

"*Tortoise*!
What comes after **16**?"

"I must know!" sobs Hare.
"The suspense is **unbearable**!"

"This wait is exhausting!
I think I'll take a nap."

1 2 3 4 5

6 7 8 9 10 11 12 13

"Oh no, I overslept!" Hare wails. "Wait, what's this?"

"**17**! How could I forget you **17**? I love you **17, 18, 19**..."

"**20**", Tortoise says.

"I knew that," says Hare.

"Now, let's count backwards! **20, 19, 18, 17, 16...**"

"Hold on, I'm coming!" says Tortoise. "**15, 14, 13, 12...**"

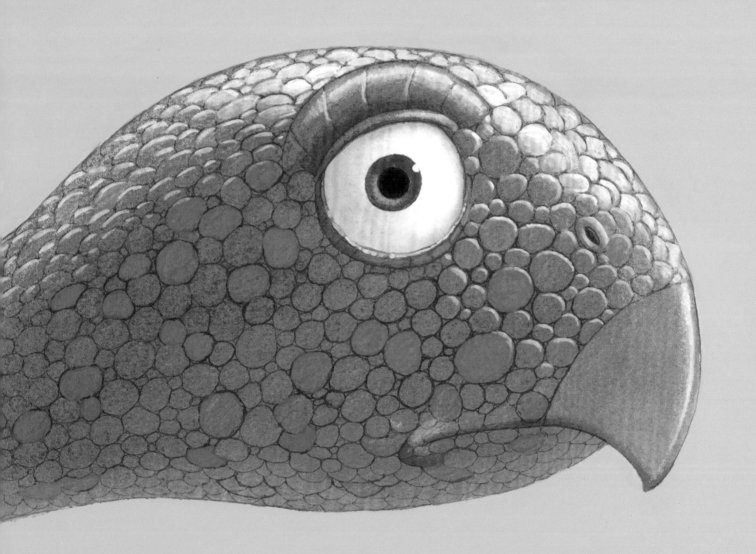